D0471430

Camille
and the SUNFLOWERS

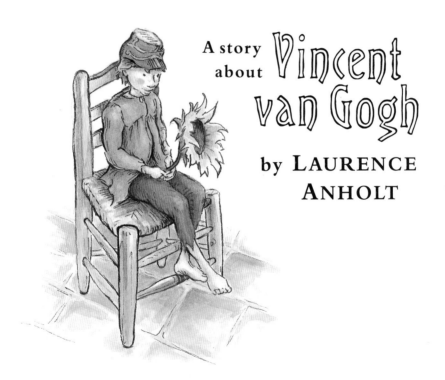

A story about **Vincent van Gogh**

by LAURENCE ANHOLT

BARRON'S

WHERE Camille lived, the sunflowers
grew so high they looked like real suns —

a whole field of burning yellow suns.

Every day after school Camille
ran through the sunflowers to meet
his father, who was a postman.
Together they would lift down
the heavy sacks of mail.

One day a strange man
arrived in Camille's town.
He had a straw hat, a yellow
beard, and quick brown eyes.

"I am Vincent, the painter," he said, smiling at Camille.

Vincent came to live in the yellow house at the end of Camille's street.

He had no money and no friends.

"Let's try to help him," said Camille's father.

So they loaded the cart with pots and pans and furniture for the yellow house.

Camille picked a huge bunch
of sunflowers for the painter and
put them in a big brown pot.

Vincent was very pleased to
have two good friends.

Vincent asked Camille's father if he would like to have his picture painted dressed in his best blue uniform.

"You must sit very still," said Vincent.

Camille loved the bright colors Vincent used and the strong smell of paint.

As Camille watched, his father's face
appeared like magic on the canvas.

The picture was strange but very beautiful.

Vincent said he would like
to paint the whole family —

Camille's mother,

his big brother,

his baby sister,...

and at last, Camille himself.

Camille was very excited — he had never even had his picture taken with a camera.

Camille took his painting to school.
He wanted everyone to see it.

But the other children didn't like
the picture. They all began to laugh.

This made Camille feel very sad.

After school some of the older
children started teasing Vincent.

They ran along behind him as
he went out to paint.

Even the grown-ups joined in.
"It's time he got a real job,"
they said, "instead of playing
with paints all day."

Camille sat for hours watching Vincent work. It was very hot but Vincent worked fast. He painted the sunflower fields and even the sun itself.

"He is the Sunflower Man," said Camille to himself.

But no matter how hard Vincent worked,
he could never sell any of his paintings.

"If I had a lot of money," said Camille,
"I would like to buy them all."

"Thank you, my friend," laughed Vincent.

One afternoon, as Camille and Vincent were coming back from the fields, some of the children from Camille's school were waiting.

They shouted at Vincent and threw stones at him.

Camille wanted them to stop — but what could he do? He was only a small boy. At last he ran home in tears.

"Listen, Camille," said his father, "people often laugh at things that are different, but I've got a feeling that one day they will learn to love Vincent's paintings."

That night, Camille
had a strange dream.
He saw Vincent standing
in the moonlight
high above the town.

Vincent had stuck candles on
his hat so that he could see.

The Sunflower Man
was painting the stars!

Early the next morning, Camille was
awakened by a loud knocking at the door.

Some men from the town had come to
see his father.

"Listen, Postman," they said,
"we want you to give this letter
to your friend. It says he must pack
up his paints and leave our town."

Camille slipped out through the
back door. He ran down the street
to the yellow house.

It seemed very quiet inside.

Then Camille saw the sunflowers he had
picked for Vincent — they had all dried
up and died. Camille felt sadder than ever.

Vincent was upstairs packing his bags.
He looked very tired but he smiled
at Camille.

"Don't be sad," he said. "It's time
for me to paint somewhere else now.
Perhaps they will like my paintings there."

"But first I have something to show you...."

Vincent lifted down a big picture.
There were Camille's sunflowers,
bigger and brighter than ever!

Camille looked at the painting.
Then he smiled too.

"Goodbye, Sunflower Man,"
he whispered, and ran out of the
yellow house and into the sunshine.

Camille's father was right. People did learn to love Vincent's paintings. Today you would have to have a lot of money if you wanted to buy one. But now people all over the world go to museums and galleries just to see Vincent's paintings of *The Yellow House*, of Camille and his family, and especially the picture of *The Sunflowers* — so bright and yellow, they look like real suns.